Little Leo Can't Sleep

Written by Mark Segal
Illustrated by Nancy Segal

Published by Orange Hat Publishing 2020

ISBN 978-1-64538-195-2

Little Leo Can't Sleep

Written by Mark Segal

Illustrated by Nancy Segal

www.orangehatpublishing.com

For Leo Robert

Our loving grandson

"Mommy Lion, I am so tired. I didn't sleep the whole night," said Little Leo.

"Oh my Little Leo, you have to try harder. Sleep is very important because it helps you grow big and strong," Mommy Lion explained.

Little Leo answered, "I try every night Mommy Lion, but I stay awake thinking of all the fun I am missing."

"Well, I understand, I understand my Little Leo. But did you know that sleep actually makes you have more fun? The more you sleep, the more fun you will have the next day," Mommy Lion said.

Little Leo went to bed the next night thinking about what Mommy Lion said. He knew it was true that sleep was of the utmost importance. But as much as he tried, sleep would not come to him.

Little Leo would have to figure out the best way to sleep.

By morning, Little Leo had a plan. He asked Mommy Lion to pack his backpack because he would be gone most of the day.

Little Leo left his home. He walked
for miles until he reached his destination.

Little Leo saw his friend Harry the Horse.

"Harry the Horse, would you please tell me how you sleep at night?" asked Little Leo.

Harry the Horse said, "I sleep standing up."

That night, Little Leo tried to sleep standing up like his friend Harry the Horse.

But that did not work. All Little Leo did was end up with sore feet.

The next day, Little Leo took another journey to ask his good friend Maria the Monkey about the best way to sleep.

"Maria the Monkey, will you please tell me how you sleep at night?" asked Little Leo.

Maria the Monkey replied, "I sleep on a branch in a tree."

Little Leo was excited to try sleeping on a branch in a tree that night.

But that did not work either. Poor Little Leo kept falling to the ground.

The next day, Little Leo went once again in search of the best way to sleep.

After a long walk, Little Leo reached the shore, where he met his friend Donnie the Dolphin.

"Donnie the Dolphin, will you please tell me how you sleep at night?" asked Little Leo.

"I sleep with one eye open," answered Donnie the Dolphin.

Little Leo was excited to try sleeping with one eye open that night.

But that did not work. All Little Leo did was stare at his stuffed animal the entire night.

Little Leo was very frustrated. He thought his wonderful idea would solve his sleeping problem, but trying to sleep like his friends did not help. He did not know what to do.

Suddenly, Little Leo heard a buzzing noise up in the sky. He looked up and saw an old friend of the family. Leo shouted,

"Ava the Bee!

Ava the Bee!"

Ava the Bee was the smartest creature in the world. Ava the Bee would know the answer.

Everyone loved Ava the Bee.

Ava the Bee buzzed down from the sky and asked, "Little Leo, why are you so upset?"

Little Leo cried, "I can't sleep. I can't sleep."

"I went to visit all my animal friends to see how they sleep, but it did not help."

Ava the Bee smiled and said in a kind and gentle way, "Oh Little Leo, I will tell you the secret to a good night's sleep."

"The idea of asking your animal friends how they fall asleep was a brilliant first step."

"But the secret is not how your animal friends fall asleep. Instead, it is why they fall asleep."

"Little Leo, let me explain why your animal friends sleep so well."

"Harry the Horse has a full stomach from eating grass in the fields all day."

"Maria the Monkey is exhausted from jumping in the trees and swinging from the branches."

"And Donnie the Dolphin relaxes all day, drifting in the beautiful blue ocean."

Little Leo thought about what Ava the Bee said.

Ava the Bee then explained, "Eating well, getting exercise, and learning to relax are very important to a good night's sleep."

"Thank you Ava the Bee, for this most important lesson," Little Leo said happily.

"I understand now. I understand now," thought Little Leo.

He then wrote Ava the Bee's instructions on his clipboard.

The next day, Little Leo ate a big breakfast, a big lunch, and a big steak dinner.

He did fifty jumping jacks and lifted weights.

And after a relaxing bath in the stream, he got ready for bed.

That night, Mommy Lion hugged Little Leo and kissed him goodnight.

Little Leo snuggled with Mommy Lion and thought about Donnie the Dolphin relaxing in the ocean.

"Sleep well Little Leo," whispered Mommy Lion. Little Leo was soon asleep.

THE END